Fergie

This story was made with the secret ingredient
of my family and friends.

Forever Rely on God,

Fran Bussard

A portion of the profit from this book is donated to:
Emerald Coast Wildlife Refuge, Inc.

WestBow Press books may be ordered through booksellers or by contacting:

WestBow Press
A Division of Thomas Nelson & Zondervan
1663 Liberty Drive
Bloomington, IN 47403
www.westbowpress.com
1 (866) 928-1240

ISBN: 978-1-9736-4398-2 (sc)
ISBN: 978-1-9736-4401-9 (e)

Library of Congress Control Number: 2018913368

Print information available on the last page.

WestBow Press rev. date: 11/15/2018

WestBow
PRESS®
A DIVISION OF THOMAS NELSON
& ZONDERVAN

Fergie

Read it, love it, share it.
Return to:

_____

Written and Illustrated by
Fran Bussard

Fergie the frog lives on a Coastal Dune Lake in Walton County, Florida. He isn't originally from there; he happened to arrive tucked inside a backpack. Was it yours? He likes the salty air and breezes that come from the Gulf of Mexico. It makes him feel like he's on vacation.

Fergie spends his days sitting, leaping, hopping, plopping, and ribbiting. He especially likes to ribbit all day...and into the night. This is just what frogs do. Ribbit, ribbit, ribbit. Do you ribbit too?

Fergie hops along the lake as he greets his friends:

"Hi-ya Dancy Dragonfly," Fergie croaks as she lands on his head.

"Where have you been hiding, Ladybug Lydia?"

"Buzz, buzz, buzz."

"Byron Bumblebee is that you?"

"Greetings Francis, the Praying Mantis."

"Long time, no see, Shadow." (Not his shadow, but a dog named Shadow, who lives in a house on the Western Lake.) Lucky dog!

"Hola, que pasa?" (Hello, what's up?) Fergie Ribbits.

Zirlinda Monarch stretches her wings wide, as she flutters, "We're headed to our family tree house to spend the winter in Mexico."

"That's a long flight over the Gulf. Via con Dios, amiga mía" (Go with God, my friend).

The view of the lake from Fergie's pad is so good, he can see and hear all the happenings. This makes every day an adventure. Do you see the red, yellow and blue fish in the lake? They're keeping their cool splashing around. Swimming and playing. Just like you!

Harry and Henrietta Heron love the wetland environment of the Coastal Dune Lake. They are gathering twigs for their nest in the tall pines. "Hurry, Harry, no time to waste," squawks Henrietta. Her clutch of eggs is due next week.

Soon after giving her the low down on where to find the twigs, Harry calls back, "Follow the leader!"

The Coastal Dune Lake isn't quiet. Just listen...you will hear the dragonflies humming as their wings flicker and flutter in the bright sunlight. Growing up in the lake, as young nymphs, they depend on the clean water for food. When dragonflies get their wings, as adults, they eat right out of the air. I bet it tastes salty!

Dancy Dragonfly hums a catchy tune as she flies higgledy-piggledy, forward, backward, and sideways. You can hear her when she hovers in place, "My name is Dancy, my wings are fancy. Up, down, all around, swinging like a chimpanzee. Watch me fly on the lake by the sea."

Francis Mantis appears to be praying as he kneels near Fergie. The critters are always curious about him since it is said that he speaks to the Great King on the wind.

"Are you talking to the King?" Ribbits Fergie.

"I am asking for His help," replies Francis.

"Did you know the Great King made you with his greatness? He is always ready to help *everyone*."

Doubting, Francis mutters, "Yakety-yak."

"No, seriously, He's got your back!" Fergie asserts.

"You seem to know a lot about the King," responds Francis.

Shadow goes down to the lake to sniff out all the sweet smells. While he and Fergie talk, Shadow gets an idea, "Let's have a party to celebrate the Great King!"

"I'll send out the invitations."

"Don't forget the R.S.V.P. We'll have a feast of treats!" Shadow always wants a bite to eat, but there is more in his furry head than what meets the eye.

Ladybug Lydia hears them as she sits on a blade of sea grass. "I do love a party, but I will not be able to come," she states sadly.

"Why not?" Ribbits Fergie.

"I'm afraid my spots are not pretty."

Smiling at Lydia, Fergie hops off his lily pad. "Don't you know your spots are beauty marks? Look at my feet. See how they are webbed? The Great King created each of us differently. That's what makes us who we are...*we're* beautiful!"

Lydia never thought of her spots like that before. Her heart shaped face smiles, "You're *right*! They are beauty marks." So, Fergie convinced Lydia to join their friends on the lake to celebrate the King.

The party begins, and Fergie ribbits stories about the Great King. While wagging his tail, Shadow encourages his friend as he retells some of their old favorites. "Right on, bring it strong. WooooooOO!" The critters discover they are one big family. You are family too.

Feeling quite festive, the raggle-taggle bunch, start to whoop it up.
Dancy Dragonfly leads them in a song, "We are the critters that glitter.
Ding a ling a ling, all our wings have bling! Ding a ling a ping ting,
sing to the King."

The happy-clappy sound reaches the Great King's ears. It melts His heart. He likes to be with his family more than anything else. Suddenly, a gust of wind blows, and Lydia spots His crown through the clouds. "The King is coming!"

Lydia is excited to meet the King she has heard so much about.
She flies up to greet Him, "I knew you'd be here!"
He looks at her spots and grins. Lydia realizes he'd always been near.
Satisfied, Fergie ribbits, "The party's complete."
"*Now*, can we eat?" Woof, woof.
The Great King laughs as they all chime in.

To their surprise, the King begins handing out gifts. They each receive just the right present.

"Awesome, a golden key!" Ladybug Lydia exclaims.

"Ribbit, ribbit, ribbit... grooo-*vy*."

"A Honey Suckle Vine...it's divine!" Blurts Baron Bumblebee.

"A new tune to sing, it's better than bling."

"It's just what I wanted," said Francis with glee.

"Yummy in my tummy. You're spoiling me," barks Shadow.

As the warm sunshine begins to fade and the evening breeze is stirring the trees, no one wants the celebration to end. Fergie ribbits what they are all thinking. "We're delighted with our gifts and we've gotten to know the Great King. Surely, it is better to be with Him for a minute than to spend 1,000 years on the lake!"

Fergie continues doing what he loves: sitting, leaping, hopping, plopping, and most of all, ribbiting. The gift Fergie received is helping his friends to understand the Great King.

Do you think what you like to do is your gift from the King...what might that be?

Fergie's Song

Patrick Brandon
Additional material by
Fran Bussard

About the author:

Fran Bussard is an artist living in the Panhandle of Florida.
She grew up in the New Orleans area and Pass Christian, Mississippi;
arrived in Florida with a backpack and decided to stay.

Fran grew up with a big drawing board in her house.
Her father was an artist by profession; sparking her imagination at an early age.

Fran's oldest brother, as a teenager, earned money trapping for a road side zoo.
Everything from bears to snakes were temporarily kept in the family's backyard.
His affinity for bringing home animals nurtured her fascination with all thing's 'critter'.

CPSIA information can be obtained
at www.ICGtesting.com
Printed in the USA
BVHW051337301118
534357BV00004B/64/P